Simon & Schuster Books for Young Readers
An imprint of Simon & Schuster Children's Publishing Division
1230 Avenue of the Americas
New York, New York 10020
Text copyright © 1998 by Frances Lincoln Limited
For photographic acknowledgments and copyright details,
see pages 72-76

First published in Great Britain in 1998 by Frances Lincoln Limited,
4 Torriano Mews, Torriano Avenue, London NW5 2RZ
First U.S. edition 1998

The text of this book is set in Perpetua.
Printed and bound in Hong Kong
10 9 8 7 6 5 4 3 2 1
Library of Congress Cataloging-in-Publication Data

Bible. O.T. Proverbs. English. Authorized. Selections. 1998.
A family treasury of proverbs.
p.   cm.
Summary: A collection of proverbs from the Biblical books of
Proverbs, Ecclesiastes, and Ecclesiasticus, illustrated by
masterworks from art museums around the world.
ISBN 0-689-82075-5
1. Bible. O.T. Proverbs—Illustrations—Juvenile literature.
2.   Bible. O.T. Ecclesiastes—Illustrations—Juvenile literature.
3.   Bible. O.T. Apocrypha. Ecclesiasticus—Illustrations—Juvenile
literature.   [1. Proverbs.   2. Bible—Selections.]   I. Bible.
O.T. Ecclesiastes. English. Authorized. Selections. 1998.
II. Bible. O.T. Apocrypha. Ecclesiasticus. English. Authorized.
Selections. 1998. III. Title.
BS1465.5.B53   1998
224.7052034—dc21   97-37209

A FAMILY TREASURY
OF PROVERBS

SIMON & SCHUSTER
BOOKS FOR YOUNG READERS

A word fitly spoken is like apples
of gold in pictures of silver.

CONTENTS

DAILY LIFE

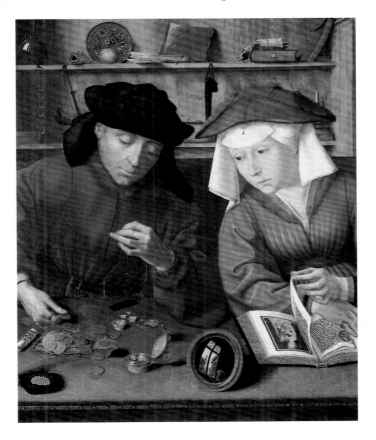

Buy the truth, and sell it not;
also wisdom, and instruction,
and understanding.

As cold waters to a thirsty soul,
   so is good news from a far country.

ECCLESIASTES 11:1

Cast thy bread upon the waters:
   for thou shalt find it after many days.

PROVERBS 16:18

Pride goeth before destruction,
and an haughty spirit before a fall.

Commend not a man for his beauty;
neither abhor a man for his outward
appearance.
The bee is little among such as fly;
but her fruit is the chief of sweet things.

Favor is deceitful, and beauty is vain:
   but a woman that feareth the Lord,
   she shall be praised.
Give her of the fruit of her hands; and let
   her own works praise her in the gates.

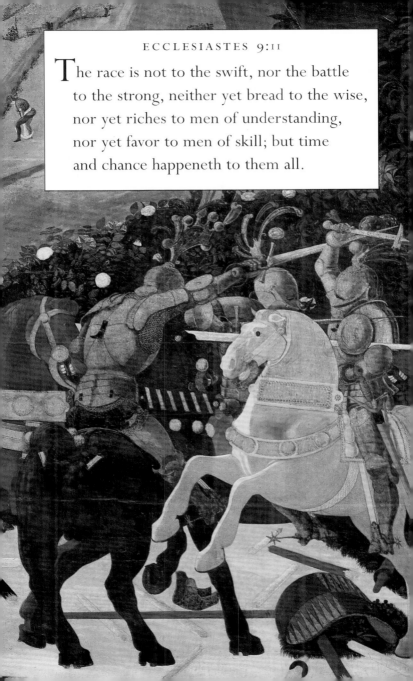

ECCLESIASTES 9:11

The race is not to the swift, nor the battle to the strong, neither yet bread to the wise, nor yet riches to men of understanding, nor yet favor to men of skill; but time and chance happeneth to them all.

Slothfulness casteth into a deep sleep;
and an idle soul shall suffer hunger.

PROVERBS 6:6

Go to the ant, thou sluggard;
consider her ways, and be wise.

PROVERBS 26:14

As the door turneth upon his hinges,
so doth the slothful upon his bed.

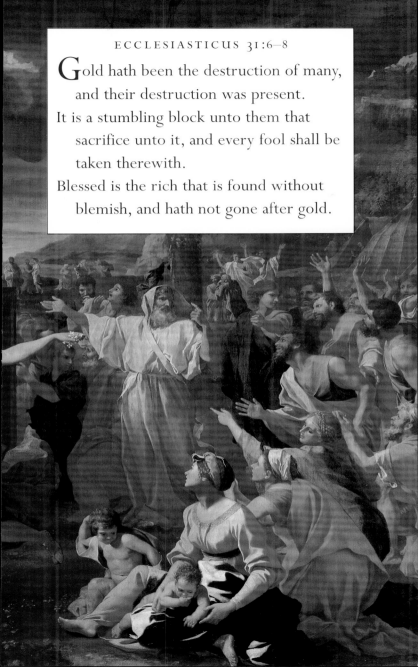

ECCLESIASTICUS 31:6–8

Gold hath been the destruction of many, and their destruction was present.

It is a stumbling block unto them that sacrifice unto it, and every fool shall be taken therewith.

Blessed is the rich that is found without blemish, and hath not gone after gold.

LOVE,
FRIENDSHIP,
FAMILY

Children and the building of a city
continue a man's name: but a blameless
wife is counted above them both.

THE SONG OF SOLOMON 8:7

Many waters cannot quench love,
neither can the floods drown it.

A faithful friend is a strong defense:
   and he that hath found such an one
   hath found a treasure.
Nothing doth countervail a faithful friend,
   and his excellency is invaluable.
A faithful friend is the medicine of life;
   and they that fear the Lord shall find him.
Whoso feareth the Lord shall direct his
   friendship aright: for as he is, so shall his
   neighbor be also.

Forsake not an old friend; for the new is not
comparable to him: a new friend is as new wine;
when it is old, thou shalt drink it with pleasure.

ECCLESIASTICUS 8:19

Open not thine heart to every man,
lest he requite thee with a shrewd turn.

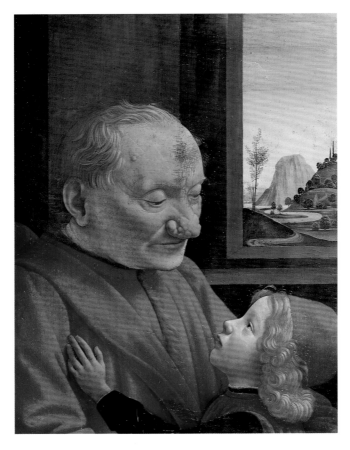

Train up a child in the way he should go: and when he is old, he will not depart from it.

The hoary head is a crown of glory,
   if it be found in the way of righteousness.

Better is a dinner of herbs where love is,
than a stalled ox and hatred therewith.

THE
PLEASURES
OF LIFE

A man hath no better thing under the sun,
than to eat, and to drink, and to be merry.

A concert of musick in a banquet of wine
  is as a signet of carbuncle set in gold.
As a signet of an emerald set in a work of gold,
  so is the melody of musick with pleasant wine.

ECCLESIASTES 5:12

The sleep of a laboring man is sweet,
whether he eat little or much.

ECCLESIASTICUS 40:22

Thine eye desireth favor and beauty:
but more than both corn while it is green.

A word spoken in due season, how good is it!

The pipe and the psaltery make sweet melody: but a pleasant tongue is above them both.

ECCLESIASTICUS 30:15

Health and good estate of body are above all gold, and a strong body above infinite wealth.

PROVERBS 15:13

A merry heart maketh
a cheerful countenance.

TIMES AND
SEASONS

To every thing there is a season, and
    a time to every purpose under the heaven:
A time to be born, and a time to die;
    a time to plant, and a time to pluck up
    that which is planted;
A time to kill, and a time to heal; a time
    to break down, and a time to build up;
A time to weep, and a time to laugh;
    a time to mourn, and a time to dance;
A time to cast away stones, and a time to
    gather stones together; a time to embrace,
    and a time to refrain from embracing;
A time to get, and a time to lose; a time
    to keep, and a time to cast away;
A time to rend, and a time to sew; a time
    to keep silence, and a time to speak;
A time to love, and a time to hate; a time
    of war, and a time of peace.

ECCLESIASTES 1:9

There is no new thing under the sun.

Be not slow to visit the sick: for that shall make thee to be beloved.

ECCLESIASTICUS 7:34

Fail not to be with them that weep, and mourn with them that mourn.

ECCLESIASTICUS 11:28

Judge none blessed before his death: for a man shall be known in his children.

What profit hath a man of all his labor
which he taketh under the sun?

One generation passeth away, and another
generation cometh: but the earth
abideth for ever.

The sun also ariseth, and the sun goeth down,
and hasteth to his place where he arose.

The wind goeth toward the south, and
turneth about unto the north; it whirleth
about continually, and the wind returneth
again according to his circuits.

All the rivers run into the sea; yet the sea is
not full; unto the place from whence
the rivers come, thither they return again.

THE PURSUIT
OF VIRTUE

A good name is rather to be chosen
than great riches, and loving favor
rather than silver and gold.

Who can find a virtuous woman?
for her price is far above rubies.
The heart of her husband doth safely
trust in her, so that he shall have no
need of spoil…
Strength and honor are her clothing;
and she shall rejoice in time to come.
She openeth her mouth with wisdom;
and in her tongue is the law of kindness.
She looketh well to the ways of her
household, and eateth not the bread
of idleness.
Her children arise up, and call her blessed;
her husband also, and he praiseth her.

ECCLESIASTES 12:13

Fear God, and keep his commandments: for this is the whole duty of man.

Strive for the truth unto death,
  and the Lord shall fight for thee.

PROVERBS 25:28

He that hath no rule over his own spirit
is like a city that is broken down,
and without walls.

WISDOM
AND FOLLY

Happy is the man that findeth wisdom,
    and the man that getteth understanding.
For the merchandise of it is better
    than the merchandise of silver,
    and the gain thereof than fine gold.
She is more precious than rubies:
    and all the things thou canst desire
    are not to be compared unto her.
Length of days is in her right hand;
    and in her left hand riches and honor.
Her ways are ways of pleasantness,
    and all her paths are peace.
She is a tree of life to them that lay hold
    upon her: and happy is every one that
    retaineth her.

Blame not before thou hast examined the truth:
understand first, and then rebuke.

Without eyes thou shalt want light:
profess not the knowledge therefore
that thou hast not.

All wisdom cometh from the Lord, and
   is with him for ever.
Who can number the sand of the sea, and
   the drops of rain, and the days of eternity?
Who can find out the height of heaven,
   and the breadth of the earth, and the deep,
   and wisdom?
Wisdom hath been created before all things,
   and the understanding of prudence
   from everlasting.
The word of God most high is the fountain
   of wisdom; and her ways are everlasting
   commandments.

Remember now thy Creator in the days of
thy youth, while the evil days come not, nor
the years draw nigh, when thou shalt say,
I have no pleasure in them.

The glory of young men is their strength:
and the beauty of old men is the gray head.

Boast not thyself of tomorrow; for thou knowest not what a day may bring forth.

Be swift to hear; and let thy life be
sincere; and with patience give answer.
If thou hast understanding, answer thy
neighbor; if not, lay thy hand upon
thy mouth.

ECCLESIASTICUS 20:2

It is much better to reprove, than to be
angry secretly: and he that confesseth
his fault shall be preserved from hurt.

PROVERBS 15:1

A soft answer turneth away wrath:
but grievous words stir up anger.

THE WISDOM OF SOLOMON 6:12

Wisdom is glorious,
and never fadeth away.

INDEX OF ARTISTS AND PAINTINGS

FRONT JACKET and PAGE 4

The Building of the
Tower of Babel *(details)*
THE BEDFORD HOURS (f.17b)
(c.1423-1430)
The British Library, London

FRONT ENDPAPERS

A Castle on the Seashore
(detail)
AMBROGIO LORENZETTI
(active 1319; died 1348/9)
Pinacoteca Nazionale, Siena

PAGE 5

Saints Peter and Dorothy *(detail)*
MASTER of the SAINT
BARTHOLOMEW ALTARPIECE
(active c.1470 to c.1510)
The National Gallery, London

PAGE 6

Rest on the Flight into
Egypt *(detail)*
ANONYMOUS NETHERLANDISH
MASTER (c.1540)
*Museo Thyssen-Bornemisza,
Madrid*

PAGE 8

The Wedding Dance
(detail)
PIETER BRUEGHEL the Elder
(active 1550/1; died 1569)
*Kunsthistorisches Museum,
Vienna*

PAGE 9

The Moneylender
and his Wife
(detail)
QUENTIN METSYS
(1466-c.1530)
Louvre, Paris

PAGE 11

The Schmadribach Falls *(detail)*
JOSEPH ANTON KOCH
(1768-1839)
*Museum der Bildenden Kunste,
Leipzig*

PAGES 12-13

The Tower of Babel *(detail)*
PIETER BRUEGHEL the Elder
(active 1550/1; died 1569)
*Kunsthistorisches Museum,
Vienna*

PAGE 14

Portrait of a Young Man
in Red *(detail)*
DOMENICO GHIRLANDAIO
(1449-1494)
The National Gallery, London

PAGE 15
Portrait of a Woman *(detail)*
ANTONIO DEL POLLAIUOLO
(c.1441-before 1496)
Galleria degli Uffizi, Florence

PAGES 16-17
The Battle of San Romano *(detail)*
PAOLO UCCELLO
(1397-1475)
The National Gallery, London

PAGE 18
Sloth *(detail)*
The Seven Deadly Sins
HIERONYMUS BOSCH
(living 1474; died 1516)
Prado, Madrid

PAGES 20-21
The Adoration of
the Golden Calf *(detail)*
NICOLAS POUSSIN
(1594-1665)
The National Gallery, London

PAGE 22
Marriage of
the Virgin *(detail)*
ROSSO FIORENTINO
(1494-1540)
San Lorenzo, Florence

PAGE 23
The Panciatichi
Holy Family
(detail)
AGNOLO BRONZINO
(1503-1572)
*Galleria degli Uffizi,
Florence*

PAGES 24-25
Christ in the Storm
on the Sea of Galilee
(detail)
JAN BRUEGHEL the Elder
(1568-1625)
*Museo Thyssen-Bornemisza,
Madrid*

PAGE 26
Saints Andrew
and Thomas
GIAN LORENZO
BERNINI
(1598-1680)
*The National
Gallery, London*

PAGE 27
The Walk
to Emmaus
(detail)
LELIO ORSI
(c.1511-1587)
*The National
Gallery, London*

PAGES 28-29
The Cheat with
the Ace of Diamonds *(detail)*
GEORGES DE LA TOUR
(1593-1652)
Louvre, Paris

PAGE 30
Portrait of an Old Man
and a Young Boy *(detail)*
DOMENICO GHIRLANDAIO
(1449-1494)
Louvre, Paris

PAGE 31
Portrait of
the Artist's Mother *(detail)*
JAMES ABBOTT McNEILL
WHISTLER (1834-1903)
Musée d'Orsay, Paris

PAGE 32
The Kitchenmaid *(detail)*
JOHANNES VERMEER
(1632-1675)
Rijksmuseum, Amsterdam

PAGE 33
The Peasant Dance *(detail)*
PIETER BRUEGHEL the Elder
(active 1550/1; died 1569)
Kunsthistorisches Museum, Vienna

PAGE 34
Boys Eating
Melons and Grapes
(detail)
BARTOLOMÉ
ESTEBAN MURILLO
(1617-1682)
*Alte Pinakothek,
Munich*

PAGE 35
A Concert
(detail)
MASTER of the FEMALE
HALF-LENGTHS
(active 2nd quarter
of 16th Century)
*The Hermitage,
St. Petersburg*

PAGES 36-37
Harvesters' Lunch
(detail)
PIETER BRUEGHEL the Younger
(c.1564-1638)
Private Collection

PAGE 38
The Visitation
(detail)
PONTORMO
(1494-1557)
San Michele,
Carmignano

PAGE 39
The Concert
(detail)
HENDRICK
TER BRUGGHEN
(c.1588-1629)
The National Gallery,
London

PAGES 40-41
Parnassus *(detail)*
ANDREA MANTEGNA
(c.1430/1-1506)
Louvre, Paris

PAGE 42
The Hunters in the Snow *(detail)*
PIETER BRUEGHEL the Elder
(active 1550/1; died 1569)
Kunsthistorisches Museum, Vienna

PAGES 44-45
The School of
Athens
(detail)
RAPHAEL
(1483-1520)
The Vatican, Rome

PAGE 47
The Death of
the Virgin
(detail)
CARAVAGGIO
(1571-1610)
Louvre, Paris

PAGES 48-49
Haymaking
(detail)
PIETER BRUEGHEL the Elder
(active 1550/1; died 1569)
Roudnice Lobkowicz Collection,
Czech Republic

PAGE 50
Saint Augustine
Leaving Rome *(detail)*
BENOZZO GOZZOLI
(c.1421-1497)
Sant'Agostino,
San Gimignano

PAGE 51
Portrait of Giovanna
Tornabuoni *(detail)*
DOMENICO GHIRLANDAIO
(1449-1494)
Museo Thyssen-Bornemisza,
Madrid

PAGE 52
The Queen of Sheba
in Adoration of the Wood *(detail)*
PIERO DELLA FRANCESCA
(1410-1492)
San Francesco, Arezzo

PAGES 54-55
Saint John the Baptist Preaching
(detail)
PIETER BRUEGHEL the Younger
(c.1564-1638)
Galerie de Jonckheere, Paris

PAGE 57
Saint George and
the Dragon *(detail)*
CARLO CRIVELLI
(c.1430/5-c.1494)
*Isabella Stewart Gardner
Museum, Boston*

PAGE 58
Saint Jerome Reading
(detail)
GIOVANNI BELLINI
(active c.1459; died 1516)
*National Gallery of Art,
Washington
(Samuel H. Kress Collection)*

PAGE 60
Christ before
the High Priest
(detail)
GERRIT VAN HONTHORST
(1592-1656)
*The National Gallery,
London*

PAGE 61
The Conversion on
the Way to Damascus
(detail)
CARAVAGGIO
(1571-1610)
*Santa Maria del Popolo,
Rome*

PAGE 62
Saint Matthew
and the Angel
(detail)
CARAVAGGIO
(1571-1610)
*San Luigi dei Francesi,
Rome*

PAGE 64
The Meeting of
Lodovico Gonzaga
and his son Cardinal
Francesco *(detail)*
ANDREA MANTEGNA
(c.1430/1-1506)
Palazzo Ducale, Mantua

PAGE 65
The Prophet
Jeremiah
(detail)
MICHELANGELO
(1475-1564)
*Sistine Chapel,
Vatican, Rome*

PAGES 66-67
The Wall with
the Guidoriccio
da Fogliano
(detail)
SIMONE MARTINI
(1284-1344)
*Palazzo Pubblico,
Siena*

PAGE 69
Predella showing Saint Peter Preaching
(detail), The Linaivoli Triptych
FRA ANGELICO
(c.1395-1455)
Museo di San Marco, Florence

PAGES 70-71 and BACK JACKET
Garden of Paradise *(detail)*
MASTER of the UPPER RHINE
(c.1415)
*Städelsches Kunstinstitut,
Frankfurt am Main*

BACK ENDPAPERS
A City on the Sea
AMBROGIO LORENZETTI
(active 1319; died 1348/9)
Pinacoteca Nazionale, Siena